This one is for Jessica May
BF

For our Billy
SW

First published in North America in 2013 by Boxer Books Limited.
First published in Great Britain in 2013 by Boxer Books Limited.
www.boxerbooks.com

The illustrations were prepared using watercolor pans and charcoal
on Aquarelle Arches hot press 180lb paper.
The text is set in Adobe Garamond.

ISBN 978-1-907967-31-3

1 3 5 7 9 10 8 6 4 2

Printed in China

All of our papers are sourced from managed forests and renewable resources.

No More Biting for Billy Goat!

Bernette Ford and Sam Williams

Boxer Books

It was Billy Goat's first day at school.

He really did not want to stay.

But Ducky came over to help him.

She always greeted anyone new.

"Let's find your play group," she said.

Billy Goat sat down, all by himself.
Bunny, Piggy, and Lambkin were
playing a game with a big ball.

Billy Goat wanted to play, too.

But he didn't know how to join them.

Ducky was watching.

"You have to ask them if you can play," whispered Ducky.

She gave Billy Goat a little nudge.

Billy Goat tugged on Bunny's sleeve.

"Can I play?" he said in a tiny whisper.

Bunny couldn't hear Billy Goat.

Billy Goat tried again.

He whispered a little louder.

Bunny didn't hear him.

So Billy Goat nipped his tail!

Bunny was startled. "Ouch!"
said Bunny. "Don't bite!"

Billy Goat tapped Lambkin's arm.

"Can I play?" he whispered.

Lambkin looked at him.

Billy Goat was getting frustrated.
So he bit Lambkin on her chubby
little arm, really hard.
"Yow-ow-ow-ow!" she cried.

Ducky ran over.

"Oh, Billy Goat," she said,

"you mustn't bite! You have to say,

in a nice strong voice,

'Please can I play with you?'"

So Billy Goat spoke up.

"Please can I play with you?"

he said to Piggy in a loud voice.

"Okay," said Piggy. "But don't bite."

Billy Goat joined the game.

But every time Piggy had the ball,

Billy Goat grabbed it away.

"No, no, no," said Piggy. "That is not the right way to play."

Billy Goat bared his little teeth.

Then he bit Piggy's ear, and he did

not let go! Piggy squealed.

"He's biting again!"

Piggy tried to run.

But Billy Goat would not let go.

Bunny and Lambkin began to cry.

Ducky ran over.

Billy Goat let go of Piggy's ear.

He started to cry, too.

He didn't like to hurt his new friends.
But he didn't know how to play the game.

"Don't cry, Billy Goat," said Ducky.

"I will help you."

Ducky taught him how to play
the new game. She helped him talk
to his new friends.

Soon it was snack time.

Now Billy Goat was using his teeth
to bite his apple, not his friends.

"No more biting for Billy Goat," he said.

Ducky put her arm around him.
"Right," said Ducky. "Teeth are
for biting food, not for biting friends."